This book belongs to...

_____

ALLEY DOGS

Barking Night

Bright ☆ Sparks

This is a Bright Sparks Book
First published in 2000
BRIGHT SPARKS, Queen Street House, 4 Queen Street, Bath BA1 1HE, UK

Copyright © PARRAGON 2000

Created and produced by THE COMPLETE WORKS,
St. Mary's Road, Royal Leamington Spa, Warwickshire CV31 1JP, UK

Editorial Director: Mike Phipps
Project Manager: Stuart Branch
Editor: Aneurin Rhys
Designer: Anne Matthews

Printed in Spain

ISBN 1-84250-004-X

ALLEY DOGS

Barking Night

Written by Lesley Rees

Illustrated by Terry Burton

Bright ☆ Sparks

It was the middle of the night.
Harvey and his gang were fast asleep in the higgledy-piggledy, messy alley, dreaming of yummy bones and chasing dustmen! The only sounds were the gentle rumblings of Ruffles' tummy and Bonnie's snores!

Everyone and everything was fast asleep — or were they?

Six naughty Alley Cats peeped over the fence. They spied the snoozing dogs and, grinning and sniggering, they scribbled and scrabbled up the fence.

"I've got an idea!" whispered Archie. "Listen..."

Wibbling and wobbling, the Alley Cats stood in a line along the top of the fence...

"Those dippy dogs are in for a fright!" giggled Archie.

"I bet I'll be the loudest!" boasted Lenny.

The cats took a deep breath, and out came the scariest, screechiest sounds you ever did hear!

The terrible noise woke Harvey with a start and made him fall off his mattress, straight on to Mac!

"What's that noise?" yelped Mac. "Is it the bagpipe ghost?"

"G-Ghost?" cried Puddles, rushing up to Harvey. "Help!"

The noise made Patchy and Ruffles jump. They fell in a big heap on top of Ruffles' bed! "Save us!" they cried.

Harvey spotted the culprits. "Oh, it's just those pesky pussies," he groaned, "up to mischief as usual. Don't worry, everyone, let's just ignore them and go back to sleep."

But those naughty cats weren't finished yet!

"Look!" cried Lenny. "One of them is still asleep. We must try harder."

They were right — Bonnie was still snoring in her dustbin!

"Louder! Louder!" screeched Archie to the others. But could they wake Bonnie? Oh no! She just kept on snoring and snoring and snoring!

"Someone should teach those cats a lesson," growled Mac. "When I was a pup I'd..."

"*Not now, Mac*," shouted the others.

Harvey smiled. He had an idea. The gang huddled together and listened.

"And me! And me!" cried Puddles, squeezing herself in.

The cats thought they were so clever. They laughed and wailed even louder!

Then suddenly, Lenny slipped and grabbed Lulu, who grabbed Hattie, who grabbed Bertie, who grabbed Lucy, who grabbed Archie – and they all tumbled headfirst into the pile of boxes and bins!

"Bravo!" woofed the dogs. "More! More!"

The cats squealed and wailed and ran away.
They'd had enough of playing tricks for one day!

"Now to get our own back," chuckled Harvey.

The gang sneaked along the alley as quiet as little mice.

"Ready?" whispered Harvey. "Steady — GO!"

"WOOF! WOOF!"

The ground shook and the cats jumped high into the air.

"Ha-ha!" roared the dogs. "Scaredy cats! Scaredy cats! We've got our own back!"

"I think that's enough frights for one night!" said Harvey.

"You're right," agreed Archie, sheepishly. "Let's all go back to bed. No more tricks tonight."

Just then Bonnie woke up. "Is it '*time-to-get-up*' time?" she asked, rubbing her eyes.

"No!" said Patchy, "it's '*time-for-bed*' time!" and they all laughed and laughed.

"Oh, goody!" yawned Bonnie. "Bedtime! The best time of the day!"

"Oh, Bonnie," smiled Harvey. "What a sleepyhead you are!"

But Bonnie didn't care. With another enormous yawn and a stretch, she turned away and wandered back to her dustbin — she was *soooo* tired!

At last the cats and dogs of the higgledy-piggledy, messy alley snuggled down to sleep, dreaming of yummy bones and chasing dustbin men — and bowls of scrummy fish! The only sounds were the rumblings of Ruffles' tummy and Bonnie's snores.

Everyone and everything was fast asleep — or were they?

"TOOWHIT – TOOWHOO!"

The End

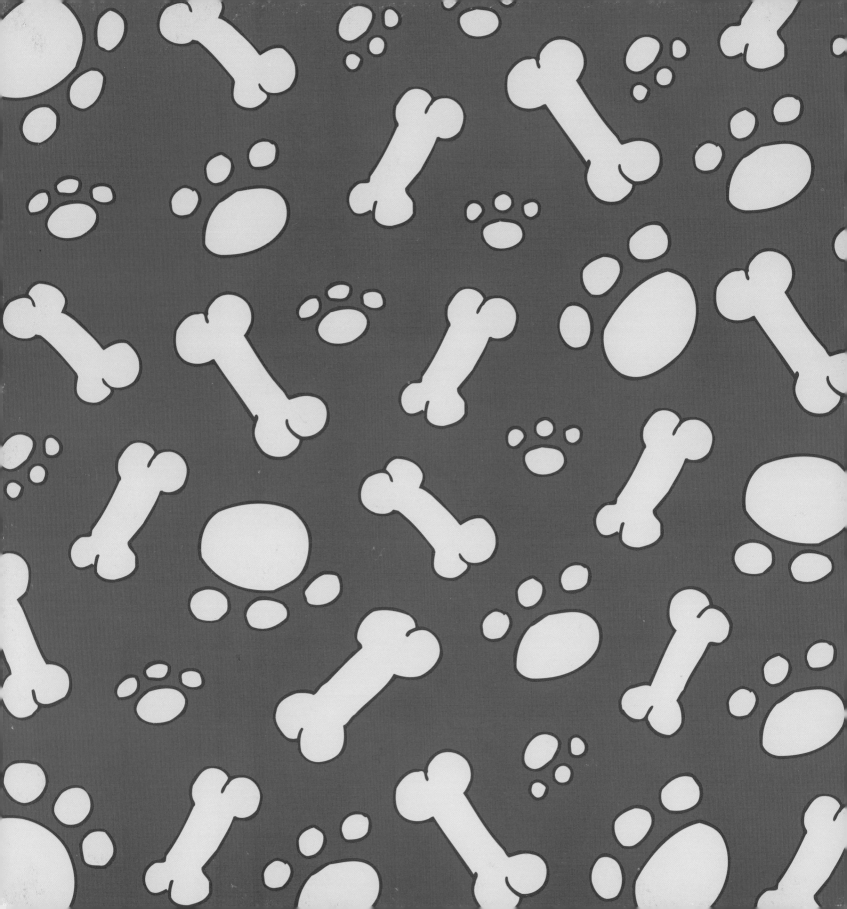